The Tiara Club

Princess Parade

For the little princesses
Sarah, Eilidh and Mhairi
x x x VF
With very special thanks to JD

www.tiaraclub.co.uk

ORCHARD BOOKS
338 Euston Road, London NW1 3BH
Orchard Books Australia
Level 17/207 Kent St, Sydney, NSW 2000

A Paperback Original
First published in Great Britain in 2007
Text copyright © Vivian French 2007
Cover illustration copyright © Sarah Gibb 2007
Inside illustrations copyright © Orchard Books 2007

The right of Vivian French to be identified as the author of this work
has been asserted by her in accordance with Copyright, Designs
and Patents Act, 1988.

A CIP catalogue record for this book is available
from the British Library.

ISBN 978 1 84616 504 7

1 3 5 7 9 10 8 6 4 2

Printed in Great Britain

The paper and board used in this paperback are natural recyclable
products made from wood grown in sustainable forests.
The manufacturing processes conform to the environmental
regulations of the country of origin.

Orchard Books is a division of Hachette Children's Books,
an Hachette Livre UK company.

www.orchardbooks.co.uk

The Tiara Club

Princess Parade

By Vivian French

ORCHARD BOOKS

The Royal Palace Academy
for the Preparation of Perfect Princesses

(Known to our students as "*The Princess Academy*")

OUR SCHOOL MOTTO:
*A Perfect Princess always thinks of others
before herself, and is kind, caring and truthful.*

**Pearl Palace offers a complete education for
Tiara Club princesses with emphasis on the arts
and outdoor activities. The curriculum includes:**

*A special Princess
Sports Day*

*A trip to the Magical
Mountains*

*Preparation for the
Silver Swan Award
(stories and poems)*

*A visit to the King
Rudolfo's Exhibition of
Musical Instruments*

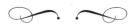

**Our headteacher, King Everest, is present at all times,
and students are well looked after by the head fairy
godmother, Fairy G, and her assistant, Fairy Angora.**

Our resident staff and visiting experts include:

*QUEEN MOLLY
(Sports and games)*

*LADY MALVEENA
(Secretary to King Everest)*

*LORD HENRY
(Natural History)*

*QUEEN MOTHER MATILDA
(Etiquette, Posture and
Flower Arranging)*

We award tiara points to encourage our Tiara Club princesses towards the next level. All princesses who win enough points at Pearl Palace will be presented with their Pearl Sashes and attend a celebration ball.

Pearl Sash Tiara Club princesses are invited to go on to Emerald Castle, our very special residence for Perfect Princesses, where they may continue their education at a higher level.

PLEASE NOTE:
Pets are not allowed at Pearl Palace. Princesses are expected to arrive at the Academy with a *minimum* of:

Twenty ballgowns (with all necessary hoops, petticoats, etc)

Twelve day dresses

Seven gowns suitable for garden parties, and other special day occasions

Twelve tiaras

Dancing shoes five pairs

Velvet slippers three pairs

Riding boots two pairs

Cloaks, muffs, stoles, gloves and other essential accessories as required

Hi, I'm SO excited I can hardly speak!
It's nearly the end of term, and
we're going to have such fun.
Isabella, Lucy, Grace, Ellie, Sarah
and I hardly slept a wink
last night in Lily Room.
Oh - I'm so silly - I haven't
told you who I am!
I'm Princess Hannah, and I'm really
REALLY pleased you're here too.
Are you ready to party?

Chapter One

Do you have a favourite teacher at your school? I do – it's Fairy G. She's the school fairy godmother, and she looks after us as well as taking some of our lessons. She's SUCH fun – except when she gets angry.

It was Fairy G who told us about the Christmas Fair. We were finishing breakfast, and she came stomping into the dining hall to join us.

"I've something very exciting to tell you," she announced as she sat down. "We've decided to hold a Pearl Palace Christmas Fair to raise money for a new charity that King Everest very much wants to help – The Twilight Home for Ancient Dragons."

At once everyone began talking, and Fairy G had to bellow, "SILENCE!" She didn't look cross, though. Her eyes were twinkling as she said, "Each room from Pearl Palace will be given a stall, and it's up to you what you sell. Or you might like to run an activity instead – something like a coconut shy, or a hoop-la stall."

"Please! Please, Fairy G!" Diamonde put up her hand and waved it madly.

"What is it?" Fairy G asked.

"Are we supposed to spend our own money?" Diamonde wanted to know. "Do we have to buy the things to sell?"

Fairy G frowned. "Certainly not," she said. "That's not at all what King Everest has in mind.

He would like you to make everything yourselves, because that way you will be making a personal contribution."

Ellie put her hand up next. "Please, Fairy G, who will come to the fair to buy what we make?"

"A very sensible question, Ellie." Fairy G beamed. "We'll invite the princesses from all the other levels in the Princess Academy – Silver Towers, Ruby Mansions, Emerald Castle, Diamond Turrets and the rest."

"WOW!" Ellie gasped. "There'll be LOADS of princesses!"

"And hopefully we'll do well enough to pay for the Twilight Home to run for many years," Fairy G said. "Now, if there are no other questions—" And she got up.

Diamonde waved her hand again. "Will there be a prize for the stall that makes the most money?"

Fairy G didn't look at all pleased. "Yes, Diamonde – although I HAD hoped you would do your best without worrying about prizes. The Twilight Home will be run by King Percival, and he's arranged a very special event.

He'd like the princesses who make the most money for the dragons to lead a Princess Parade on the opening day, and to cut a ribbon of stars before declaring the home open."

Diamonde sniffed. "Well, THAT doesn't sound very special."

Fairy G gave Diamonde a chilly stare. "'A Perfect Princess works her hardest for the sake of others, not for a reward or prizes!'"

As soon as breakfast was over we had a *How to Choose the Perfect Menu* lesson with Lady Malveena, so we couldn't talk about the Christmas Fair, but the second the bell rang for break we rushed into the garden.

"Shall we make some fantastic cakes?" Isabella asked.

"We'd have to make an awful lot." Sarah rubbed her nose thoughtfully. "What about a game?"

"That could be fun," Ellie said.

Isabella nodded. "Has anyone got any ideas?"

"Maybe it could be something

to do with dragons and Christmas?" I suggested.

"BRILLIANT!" Grace patted me on the back. "Like what?"

My brain went totally blank. "Erm...I can't quite think at the moment," I said.

Lucy's eyes began to sparkle.

"Hey! What about 'Pin the Tail on the Dragon'?"

"They've got awfully long tails," Isabella pointed out. "Mightn't that be too easy?"

"Mmm," Lucy said. "Perhaps you're right."

There was a silence while we all thought as hard as we could.

"Why! It's the loopy Lilies!" Diamonde and Gruella walked past us, looking very pleased with themselves.

"We've had an AMAZING idea for the fair," Diamonde called over her shoulder.

"Actually," I told her, "we've

got a good idea too."

Diamonde stuck her nose in the air. "We'll still be the best!" And they marched away.

"Help," Grace said. "We'll have to think of something REALLY good now."

"I know!" An idea suddenly popped into my head. "We could play Feed the Dragon his Christmas Dinner! What if we make a big cardboard dragon and lots of little Christmas puddings, and people have to toss the puddings into his mouth?"

"And if they get three puddings in his mouth they get a prize!" Lucy clapped her hands. "Oh, that sounds SUCH a good idea!"

"We can make sweets for prizes," Isabella said. "And we

can make the dragon in the art room! Oh – DO let's!"

We looked at each other, our eyes shining.

"Lily Room for The Dragon's Christmas Dinner!"

As soon as break was over we hurried back into school for Dress Design (*How to Look Perfect for Every Occasion*) and found our friends had been making plans as well. Rose Room were going to make Christmas decorations, Poppy Room had decided on Christmas cards (Georgia is just

SO brilliant at drawing!), and Sunflower Room were wondering what to put on their hoop-la stall. Lavender Room were thinking about making a huge cake and asking people to guess its weight, and Daffodil Room were bouncing with excitement because they'd decided to make paper chains.

"What are Lily Room going to do?" Diamonde stared at me. "I bet it's something silly."

I tried hard not to get cross. "We've thought of a game."

"It's called The Dragon's Christmas Dinner!" Grace said cheerfully. "Are you going to tell us what you've decided?"

Diamonde tossed her head. "We're going to sell lots of pretty Christmas brooches. Little Christmas trees."

"That's a good idea." I could tell Sarah was trying not to sound surprised. "What are you going to make them out of?"

"Oh, we're not going to make them," Gruella began. "We're going to—OW!"

She stopped to rub her arm where Diamonde had pinched her.

"Why did you do that?" she asked. "It HURT!"

Diamonde smiled a false looking smile. "She's just got muddled," she told us. "Of course we're going to make them." She grabbed Gruella, and pulled her to the other side of the classroom just as Duchess Delia came sailing through the door.

"They're up to something," Sarah whispered in my ear as the duchess began to draw on the board.

I thought she was right, but I didn't dare answer. Duchess Delia hates people talking, and I SO didn't want to be given minus tiara points or a detention.

Later that day we had an art lesson, and Fairy Angora let us begin making our dragon. It was SUCH fun! We made the head really huge, but we only cut quite a small hole for the mouth.

"We don't want TOO many people winning prizes," Isabella said, and we all agreed.

Fairy Angora found us some old boxes for the body, and we spent ages cutting out cardboard spikes to make a golden spiky spine.

We decided to make the Christmas puddings like bean bags, and Lucy and Ellie said they'd go up to the sewing room after school.

"What kind of sweets shall we make for prizes?" Isabella asked as she began carefully painting the dragon's eyes.

"I can make marzipan fruit," Sarah offered. "It's really easy."

"That sounds wonderful!" I tried to think if I could make anything, but I couldn't. I am SO not good at things like that! But then I had a different idea. "What about making little dragons' eggs instead of fruit?"

"Yes!" Sarah smiled from ear to ear. "That'll be even easier! I'll go down to the kitchen when Lucy and Ellie are in the sewing room..."

"I'll help you," Grace said. "I LOVE marzipan!"

"And Isabella and I can go on working on the dragon," I said happily. "Hurrah!"

Chapter Three

Pearl Palace was absolutely BUZZING for the next few days. All of us were working away at our different projects; everybody, that is, except for Diamonde and Gruella. They didn't seem to do anything except float round making rude remarks.

"Do you think Fairy G's

noticed?" Isabella asked as we were putting the final touches to our dragon.

"I don't know," I said. "It does seem a bit odd, though."

Isabella sucked the end of her paintbrush thoughtfully. "Have you noticed how they jump every time the messengers come with letters and parcels? I know a Perfect Princess Always Thinks the Best of Others, but I can't help wondering what they're waiting for."

I was about to say, me too, when we were interrupted by Lucy and Ellie carrying a basket of the sweetest little bean bag Christmas puddings.

"Wow, those are amazing!" I told them.

Isabella picked a pudding out of the basket, and tossed it into the dragon's mouth. "Perfect!"

"Just a minute," I said, and I wriggled into the dragon's body. "Throw another one in!"

Isabella, Lucy and Ellie began to giggle, and I stuck my head out. "What's so funny?"

"Your voice sounds all hollow and boomy," Lucy explained. "JUST like a dragon!"

"Does it?" I wriggled back inside the dragon.

"RRRRRRRR! RRR!" I roared. "YOU HAVE WON A PRIZE!"

I could hear my friends shrieking with laughter, and I crawled out feeling very pleased with our invention.

"Let's go and see how Sarah and Grace are getting on," Isabella said as we took off our painting aprons. "I think we've finished here."

We were just crossing the main hall when Lady Malveena came stalking towards us. She was holding a large parcel, and for once she looked happy to see us.

"Aha! Princesses! I seem to have mislaid my spectacles, so would you be kind and tell me who this is for?"

I peered at the label. There was a massive gold crest, and a lot of very curly writing.

For the Princesses Diamonde and Gruella.

Darling girlies!
Make sure you win!
Lots of luck to my precious little sweetie birds.
Mummy

"Erm..." I said. "It's for Diamonde and Gruella."

"Thank you, Princess Hannah." Lady Malveena peered at me short-sightedly. "Could you take it to them? I really must look for my spectacles."

"Of course," I said, although I was longing to see what Sarah and Grace were up to in the kitchen. "I'll take it straight away."

I took the box, and hurried towards the recreation room. As I went I couldn't help thinking about what Isabella had said. Had Diamond and Gruella's mother REALLY sent them lots of brooches to sell?

The twins were lying on a sofa eating chocolates when I arrived, but as soon as they saw me they stuffed the box under a cushion.

"This has just come for you," I said, and I handed over the

parcel. Gruella's eyes lit up, but Diamonde looked at me suspiciously.

"How come YOU'VE got it?" she wanted to know.

I explained about Lady Malveena, and I couldn't help adding, "I hope it's something nice."

"It'll be our new dresses for the Christmas Fair," Diamonde said, but Gruella squeaked, "It's our new tiaras..."

There was a pause, and Gruella went pink. "Oh yes! It's our dresses!"

"Aren't you going to open it?" I know it was mean of me to ask, but I couldn't help it. It was mean of the twins not to make their brooches!

"We'll open it later," Diamonde said firmly, and she put the parcel in her locker. She gave me one of her false smiles. "How's your dear little dragon?"

"It's finished," I told her. "I'm just going down to the kitchen to see how Sarah and Grace are getting on."

"Ooooh!" Gruella cooed. "What are they doing there?"

I didn't particularly want to tell them about the marzipan prizes, but it seemed rude not to, so I did. And when I went down to the kitchen the twins followed me – and I couldn't help thinking they were doing everything they could to make me forget about their parcel.

Isabella, Lucy and Ellie were in the kitchen peering at two

big trays of marzipan dragons' eggs, and ooohing and ahhing because they were just wonderful.

Sarah and Grace had coloured them with swirls of blue and green and gold, and they looked far too magical to eat.

"Goodness," Gruella said. "They're REALLY pretty!"

Sarah laughed. "So are my hands – look!" She held out her

hands, and she was right - her
fingers were covered in blue and
green food colouring.

Grace giggled. "Fairy G popped
in to see how we were getting on,
and said Sarah looked like an
alien!" She pointed at a pile of
pink and blue tissue paper.

"Do you want to help wrap the eggs up?"

To my astonishment the twins actually sat down and helped us, and they didn't make a single nasty remark! By the time we'd finished I didn't know WHAT to think...but I did still feel suspicious. Somehow it was just too good to be true.

Chapter Four

On the day of the Christmas Fair we positively leapt out of bed and into our clothes.

"Wouldn't it be so brilliant if we won the prize?" Ellie said as she brushed her hair. "Just imagine leading the Princess Parade, and getting to cut a starry ribbon!"

"It would be FABULOUS," I agreed, and we hurried down the stairs to breakfast.

We'd just begun eating when Fairy G and King Everest came sweeping into the dining hall.

"Princesses!" King Everest boomed. "I have to say I am VERY proud that ALL my princesses have been working so hard. I would have been most disappointed if any of you hadn't made your own gifts and prizes." He stopped to smile at us all. "In fact, you would have been disqualified from the competition."

Beside me Diamonde and Gruella froze.

"But of course," King Everest went on, "that won't happen.

Now, as soon as breakfast is over the stalls will be set up. I will declare the Pearl Palace Christmas Fair open at twelve o'clock exactly – and may it be a HUGE success!"

I didn't know whether to look at Diamonde and Gruella or not. They were whispering furiously, and a moment later they excused themselves and disappeared. I didn't see them again until we were arranging our dragon, and to my amazement they looked really happy!

Diamonde even insisted on running down to the kitchen to fetch the basket of dragons' eggs for us.

"Thank you," I said. "And good luck with your brooches! I'd love to see them. Where's your stall?"

For a second Diamonde looked REALLY weird. "Erm – on the other side of the hall," she said, and she turned and ran.

"Hmm," Grace said as she watched her disappear. "She's

definitely up to something!"

I nodded, and thought about trying to find the twins' stall. But just then King Everest declared the Christmas Fair was open, and hundreds of princesses flooded into the Pearl Palace ballroom.

Right from the beginning our dragon was REALLY popular. Absolutely everybody wanted to have a go, but nobody won a prize until King Everest came marching up.

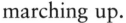

"Excellent idea!" he boomed.
"Excellent!" And he tossed three
puddings in to the dragon's mouth
with no trouble at all!

"RRRRR!" Sarah roared from
inside.

"Well done, Your Majesty," I said, and I handed him a prize wrapped in pink tissue paper. "I hope it tastes OK!"

King Everest looked pleased, and ripped it open – and out tumbled a brooch. A shiny little Christmas tree brooch – with a price label still attached.

"WHAT..." I began – and then I was silent. I knew EXACTLY what Diamonde had done, and I was raging mad – but what could I do?

Chapter Five

King Everest stared at the brooch.
"I think, Princess Hannah," he
said grimly, "you and the rest
of Lily Room had better come
with me."

"But we've never seen—" Lucy
began, but King Everest held up
his hand.

"No excuses, if you please."

He sounded furious, and Lucy, Grace, Isabella and Ellie came to stand silently beside me. "Where is Princess Sarah?"

The dragon's body heaved, and Sarah wriggled out. Her foot caught in the dragon's tail, and as she put out her hand to push the tail to one side I couldn't help smiling. Her hands were still bright blue and green! King Everest noticed as well, and his frown grew even fiercer.

"Sarah! What HAVE you been doing? NO Perfect Princess should EVER appear in public with such disgustingly dirty hands!"

Sarah blushed, and hung her head. "I'm so very sorry, Your Majesty," she whispered. "It was the food colouring from the dragons' eggs."

"EGGS? What eggs? What do you mean?" As our headteacher stared at her, another voice spoke from just behind us. Well – not so much spoke, as BOOMED!

"May I offer you a marzipan sweet, Your Majesty?"

King Everest positively jumped as Fairy G waved a handful of pink tissue paper under his nose.

"This is not the time, Fairy G," he said crossly. "These princesses have been cheating! Look! Just look at what they offered me as a prize!" And he held out the brooch.

Fairy G looked, and shook her head. "Shocking," she agreed.

"But Your Majesty – look at THESE!" She opened the tissue paper, and there were two of our beautiful dragons' eggs. "Now, can you tell me where you've seen these splendid blues and greens before? I knew as soon as I saw them!" And she gave the king a

beaming smile as she pointed to Sarah's hands.

I don't think I'd ever seen King Everest look so bewildered. "Fairy G," he said, "I have absolutely NO idea what you're trying to say!"

Fairy G sighed. "Let me explain.

Here are two blue and green marzipan dragons' eggs. Sarah has blue and green hands. Diamonde and Gruella, who were selling the eggs, have clean hands, and were quite unable to tell me how they'd made them. I find it all rather strange – don't you?"

If King Everest had looked fierce before, it was NOTHING to the way he looked now! His eyes actually flashed as he roared, "Fetch the twins!"

"No need," Fairy G told him. "I brought them with me." She moved to one side, and we saw Diamonde and Gruella standing behind her. Gruella was very pale, but Diamonde folded her arms and tried to look brave.

"It was a mistake, Your Majesty," she said quickly. "We were SO confused by the tissue paper..."

She stopped, and took a deep breath. "We didn't tell Lily Room we had their basket by mistake, because we thought they'd do better with the brooches. We were trying to help them, actually."

"I see." King Everest's voice was cold. "You didn't think Lily Room would get into trouble for not having made their prizes?"

"But they're NICE brooches, Your Majesty!" Gruella said indignantly. "Mummy got them from the BEST shop..." Her voice faded, and she hung her head.

"Diamonde and Gruella," King Everest said, "I am disappointed in you. Please go to your room, and stay there until I decide whether I should send you home or not."

As Diamonde and Gruella crept away, King Everest turned to me and my friends. "I owe you an apology, princesses," he said. "I'm very sorry to have doubted you. Please carry on with your excellent game!"

Fairy G smiled at us as our

headteacher marched off.

"Let's straighten things out," she said, and waved her wand. At once silvery sparkles floated over us, and our basket of prizes vanished – only to be replaced by another basket, and a big bowl FULL of silver pennies.

"Your marzipan eggs, and the money they earned," Fairy G said triumphantly. "Oh—" she waved her wand again, and Sarah's hands were back to normal. "We can't have a prize-winning princess with dirty hands, can we?" And she winked.

We almost stopped breathing. "Prize-winning princess?"

Fairy G nodded. "Diamonde and Gruella sold nearly every single one of your eggs! If you add that to the money you have here, I think you'll find you've done very well indeed."

"But is that fair?" I asked.

"Completely fair," Fairy G said firmly. "Now, you've got another twenty minutes before the fair ends. Enjoy yourselves!" She picked up a pudding, and threw it into the dragon's mouth.

"RRRRRRR! RRRR!" roared the dragon...

And do you know what? Not one of us was inside it! But we heard Fairy G chuckle as she walked away.

Chapter Six

Fairy G was right. We DID win the competition – we won by a long long way! But we still gasped in astonishment when King Everest announced that LILY ROOM was going to lead the parade, and cut the ribbon to open the Twilight Home for Ancient Dragons.

"We'll have to have very special dresses," Grace said as we sat up in bed in Lily Room that night.

Visit www.tiaraclub.co.uk
to download your printable palace scene.

The Tiara Club series is written by Vivian French and illustrated by Sarah Gibb. www.orchardbooks.co.uk

"VERY special," Ellie agreed.

"Do you think we'll get to ride on a dragon?" Isabella asked.

Sarah's eyes lit up. "Ooooh! That would be SO exciting!"

"What a wonderful way to end the term," Lucy sighed happily.

I thought she was absolutely right, but do you know the most exciting and truly wonderful thing of all?

We'd won because we'd all worked together...

And best of all, you were there too. Friends together!

See you at the Princess Parade!

Hello! I'm Princess Lucy!
And isn't it SO exciting?
You're going to come with us when
we open the Twilight Home for
Ancient Dragons! I'm so pleased,
because it wouldn't be the same
without you. And Hannah, Isabella,
Grace, Ellie and Sarah are thrilled too –
it's going to be SUCH fun.

Chapter One

Do you like pink? I do – it's one of my two most favourite colours. When King Everest announced that Lily Room were going to lead the Princess Parade before opening King Percival's new home for Ancient Dragons, I just knew I had to have a new pink dress. After all, it was going to be a

VERY special occasion.

"Don't you think pink velvet would be absolutely gorgeous?" I asked Hannah.

Hannah nodded. "Actually, I was thinking of wearing pink as well," she confessed.

Grace, who was sitting next to Hannah, began to giggle. "Oh no! Me too."

Ellie and Sarah looked at each other, and then Sarah said, "So were we!"

Hannah was looking thoughtful.

"Where's the Princess Parade going to be? Because if it's outside it might be chilly…"

"Good thinking," I told her. "Let's ask Fairy G. We've got time before the supper bell goes."

We jumped up from the sofa, and made our way out of the recreation room.

Diamonde and Gruella were outside, and Diamonde gave us a cold stare.

"Oh look – it's the loopy Lilies! I suppose you're SO pleased because you won the competition! But we're going to be in the parade too, and we're going to have the most beautiful dresses EVER, so there."

Gruella nodded. "That's right! Our mummy's bought us these fabulous pink dresses with lacy petticoats and—"

"SH!" Diamonde hissed, and she grabbed Gruella and dragged her away.

As they disappeared down the long corridor Sarah nudged me. "Sounds as if every princess in the parade will be dressed in pink!"

"I won't," Isabella said quietly.

"I'll have to wear my green dress. I can't ask Mum for another one."

As I turned to stare at her I suddenly realised she hadn't joined in when we were talking about our new dresses, and I felt TERRIBLE. Isabella has dozens of little brothers, and I don't think her family has any money at all.

I know she once told me the palace they live in has big cracks in the ceiling.

"Actually," I said, "I don't think pink is Christmassy enough. I might wear my hollyberry red dress instead."

Isabella shook her head. "I don't want you feeling sorry for me, Lucy. It's quite OK – I do like my green dress."

Ellie hadn't been listening to me or Isabella. "I know! Maybe we could wear different shades of pink – what do you think?"

"I told you. I've got to wear green." And Isabella went back into the recreation room, banging the door behind her.

"What did I say?" Ellie asked in surprise.

I took her arm. "She can't ask her parents for a new dress," I whispered. "I think it's because they don't have enough money."

"Oh." Ellie looked horrified. "I'm SO stupid – I never thought! Shall I go and tell her I'm sorry?"

I didn't answer. An idea was growing inside my mind, and I wanted to see if it really was as good as I thought it was.

"What about," I said slowly, "what about NONE of us having new dresses? What if we asked Fairy G to help us make over our old dresses – and then Isabella wouldn't feel left out?"

"BRILLIANT!" Grace clapped her hands, but Hannah looked doubtful.

"She'll think we're doing it because we're sorry for her," she said, "and she'll hate it."

"No she won't." I began to smile. "That's the best bit of my plan. We'll ask our parents to give some of the money they'd have spent on our dresses to the Twilight Home. So we can tell Isabella we're not doing it for her – it's for the dragons!"

There was a little pause, and then Ellie said, "Well done, Lucy! Shall we tell Isabella now, or wait until later?"

"Now," I said, and we opened the recreation room door.

Chapter Two

At first Isabella wouldn't believe we wanted to wear our old party dresses, but in the end we managed to persuade her.

"Let's have a parade in Lily Room this evening after supper," Ellie suggested, "and we'll think how we can make our dresses extra special."

Ellie LOVES sewing, and I do too, although I'm not always very good at finishing things off properly.

Isabella stopped looking droopy, and sat up. "If we go right this minute and ask Fairy G if the parade's inside or out, we can decide what we need!"

Five minutes later we were in Fairy G's study, and Fairy G was beaming at us. She's the school fairy godmother, and she's great fun. When we told her we wanted to make more money for the charity by wearing our old dresses, she was so pleased she went bright red.

"That, my dears," she told us, "only goes to show you are well on the way to becoming Perfect Princesses. Ten tiara points each!"

"Thank you!" we gasped.

Grace said, "Honestly, Fairy G –
we didn't do it because we were
hoping for tiara points."

Fairy G's eyes twinkled. "I know
that, my dear. Now, go and find
Duchess Delia, and she'll help you
to find some lovely new trimmings
and ribbons and bows. After all,

you'll be cutting the starry ribbon, and we want you to look your very best!"

"Thank you," we said again, and then I suddenly remembered why we'd come.

"Please – where will the parade be held?"

"Goodness me!" Fairy G looked most surprised. "Hasn't King Everest told you?"

We shook our heads.

"It'll be in the grounds of King Percival's lovely palace," Fairy G explained. "Up until now the ancient dragons have had to live in a horribly damp cave on the other side of the lake, poor old things. King Percival has decided the parade will begin at the cave, go round the lake, and across the gardens to the front door of the new Twilight Home. Once you reach the door you'll cut the ribbon of stars and declare the home open, and the dragons will be tucked up in comfort just in time for Christmas. Doesn't that sound wonderful?"

We didn't answer at once, as a huge question was looming in each of our minds. It was Isabella who finally asked, "Erm...do you mean we'll be parading with DRAGONS?"

Fairy G laughed her enormous booming laugh. "Of course! What did you expect?"

We looked at each other, and I had to swallow hard before I could ask, "Are they...are they SAFE?"

"Safe as houses," Fairy G said cheerfully. "Besides, King Percival will be in charge of everything. No need to worry, no need at all. Now, hurry along and ask

Duchess Delia what she can find you, and make sure you have a little cape or a wrap in case the weather turns cold. Although I expect the dragons could always warm you with a blast of fire!" And she chuckled as she opened her door to send us on our way.

"WOW!" Hannah very nearly exploded as we bounced out into the corridor. "I hoped we might ride on a dragon – but I never thought we'd actually get to walk beside one!"

Grace's eyes were shining. "I wonder how big they are?"

I was remembering the dragon we'd ridden on when we were in our very first term at the Princess Academy, and thinking how HUGE she'd been...and I could feel my stomach begin to do cartwheels.

Ellie smiled, and squeezed my

hand. "They're very ANCIENT dragons," she said comfortingly. "They probably can't even fly about any more."

I nodded, although it wasn't the flying I was worried about. It was the fire they breathed and the teeth and the claws.

Chapter Three

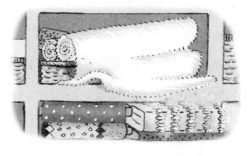

Duchess Delia wasn't in the sewing room when we got there, so we wandered round looking at all the beautiful bits and pieces she keeps in baskets on the shelves. There was a roll of absolutely adorable fluffy white fake fur, and I couldn't help thinking how wonderful it would look on the

hems and necks of our dresses.
When I mentioned it to Ellie her
eyes lit up.

"Oh, YES!" she breathed. "And
we could make some white fur
pompoms for extra decoration –
that would be SO Christmassy!
It would look like sweet little
snowballs!"

Hannah put out a hand to stroke
the fur. "It's so soft," she said. "I've
got a long dark red party dress I've
hardly ever worn because it's so
plain, but this would make it look
utterly fabulous."

Isabella nodded. "It'll look
really pretty on green as well."

"What do you think?" I asked Sarah and Grace, but I didn't need them to tell me that they loved the idea. They were smiling happily—

And then the door opened, and in swept Duchess Delia, with the twins behind her.

"Well I never!" she said. "I AM popular today! And what can I do for Lily Room?"

I opened my mouth to answer, but before I could say a word Diamonde and Gruella pushed in front of me. They were both carrying beautiful pink satin dresses, and Diamonde almost forced hers into Duchess Delia's arms.

"We asked you first," she said rudely. "You said you'd make our dresses fit!"

"That's right!" Gruella dumped her dress on top of Diamonde's.

Duchess Delia drew herself up to her full height.

"Tut tut! Princess Gruella and Princess Diamonde," she snapped. "I am NOT prepared to help ANYONE who speaks to me like that! Please take five minus tiara points, and wait over there." She pointed to a corner of the sewing room, and turned to us. "I hear

you're going to be leading the dragons to their new home, princesses. How wonderful! But do mind you don't scream. Dragons really hate screaming, you know."

"D...d...do they?" I couldn't quite stop my voice shaking.

"It's very well known." Duchess Delia sounded very certain. "It reminds them of their terrible past, when princesses used to be chained to rocks, and it upsets them dreadfully."

"We definitely won't scream," Sarah said firmly.

"A wise decision," the duchess told her. "Now, what was it you girls wanted?"

"If you please," Ellie said, "we're going to wear our old party dresses to the Princess Parade, but we'd like to put new trimming on them. Would it be possible to use some of that fake fur?"

Duchess Delia smiled. "Of course," she said. "Have you brought your dresses with you?"

We explained that we were going to try them on that evening, and the duchess promised to help us if we came back the next day. I could hear Diamonde and Gruella muttering behind us, and the moment we'd finished talking they popped out of their corner.

"Fancy not having new dresses for the special parade," Diamonde sneered. "WE have, haven't we, Gruella?"

For once Gruella didn't agree. "I wouldn't mind wearing an old dress if it had pretty fur on it," she said. "Our new dresses are much too tight."

Diamonde snorted. "They'll be fine when they've been altered." She swept Duchess Delia a curtsey, and said, "Please excuse me if I was rude. You will help us, won't you?"

Duchess Delia didn't look at all impressed by Diamonde's apology, but she agreed to alter the dresses. The twins thanked her, and followed us as we went back downstairs.

"So why aren't any of you getting new dresses?" Diamonde wanted to know.

Isabella blushed, and I said quickly, "Actually, we're saving the money so we can give some more to the Dragons' Home."

Diamonde stared, then sneered, "Ooooh! Aren't you goody-goody little princesses?"

"Yes," boomed a loud voice

from behind her. "They are good. And it would be a pleasant change if you were as kind and caring as Lily Room, Diamonde!"

And Fairy G strode past us carrying a pile of boxes and bottles.

I could almost hear Diamonde grinding her teeth, she was so furious.

"Just you wait!" she muttered. "You think you're SO wonderful – but just you wait! I'll show Fairy G and everyone just how stupid you really are!"

As she stormed off towing Gruella behind her, Grace sighed. "They never learn, do they?"

"No," I agreed, but I couldn't help wondering what horrible scheme Diamonde might dream up to get her own back.

Chapter Four

We had SUCH fun that evening. We tried on all our dresses, and decided which we wanted to wear for the parade. I chose my hollyberry red one, and Hannah found her long dark red dress, and we all agreed it would look fabulous with white fur trimming. And the next day we were allowed to spend the whole morning in the sewing room, and Duchess Delia helped us until our dresses looked prettier than we ever could have imagined.

"It's MUCH nicer than when it was brand new," Isabella said with a happy sigh as she held up

her green dress. "Look!"

"I can't wait until Saturday," I said as I stitched the little snowball bobbles onto my white fur cape.

"What about the dragons?" Ellie teased as she passed me the scissors.

"Perfect Princesses try to look brave even when they're feeling wobbly," I told her, and she giggled.

"I haven't heard that rule before," she said, "but it sounds a good one to me!"

But by Saturday lunchtime I wasn't feeling at all like a Perfect Princess. My heart was pitter-pattering dreadfully as we climbed into the coach that was going to take us to King Percival's Palace. I tried to pretend I was fine, but by the time we drew up in front of the palace I was trembling.

"Are you OK, Lucy?" Grace asked me.

I did my best to smile, but it wasn't very real, and Grace gave me a hug. "You can do it," she told me. "I know you can!"

That made me feel better, and when King Percival welcomed us into his palace I was just about able to curtsey without falling over.

"We have to wait a few moments

for the rest of the Pearl Palace princesses to arrive," the king told us. "And then I'll take you down to meet the dragons, and the parade can begin." He smiled proudly. "This is a very special day for me, my dears – a very special day. My boys are so VERY excited. They're longing to see their new home!"

I was trying hard NOT to imagine an excited dragon when I caught Ellie's eye, and she gave me a tiny wink. A moment later the rest of the coaches arrived, and I was able to take some deep breaths while King Percival, King Everest and Fairy G fussed about and told everyone where to stand. And then it was time to begin.

Chapter Five

As Lily Room were to lead the parade, we had to walk past all the other Pearl Palace princesses, and lots of our friends gave us encouraging smiles. Even Gruella gave a little wave, but Diamonde just glared at us.

"She's jealous," Sarah whispered in my ear.

I nodded; I couldn't whisper back because my heart had begun to race. We were approaching a dark opening in a heap of rocks, and a faint wisp of smoke hung in the air outside. King Percival stopped, and whistled...and out of the cave limped an amazingly old dragon, followed by five others.

Their scales were dull and dusty, and their wings were drooping, and I knew at once I wasn't frightened any more. They were looking round in an interested sort of way, but they were SO not scary. Just very old, and actually rather sad. King Percival stepped forward, and took hold of the first dragon by his lead.

"Here you are, Princess Lucy," he said. "You can lead Valiant.

Just talk to him quietly, and he'll follow you like a lamb." He handed me the long leather lead, and the dragon dropped his huge head to look at me. His eyes were surprisingly clear, and we looked at each other for what seemed like a long time.

"Hello," I said. "Hello, Lord Valiant." And I don't know what made me say it, but I went on, "I feel very honoured to be walking beside you to your new home."

"Good girl," King Percival said softly. "Now, walk him slowly down the path, and the others will follow after him."

So I began to walk, and Valiant

walked beside me, and all the time I talked to him and told him how wonderful I thought he was, and how I'd never expected to meet such a fabulous dragon, and what extraordinary things he must have seen and done. The other dragons walked steadily behind us, and we paraded away from the cave towards the lake.

And then—

"AYEEEEEEEEEEEEEEEEEEE EEEEEEE!"

There was the most piercing scream, and the dragons jumped. Valiant threw his head in the air, and I almost let go of the lead as he let out a HUMUNGOUS roar. Flames soared into the sky followed by a thick cloud of black smoke. My heart leapt into my mouth, and I went cold all over – and then I understood. He wasn't angry. He was scared – really scared. I could feel him trembling all over as he roared, just like I'd been trembling on the coach.

And I remembered how Grace had hugged me, so I put my hand on his side.

"It's all right, Valiant," I called, "it's only a horrible noise. Truly it is. Remember what a strong and wonderful dragon you are, and don't let it frighten you. You can do it! I know you can!"

For a moment I honestly thought he was going to tear the lead out of my hands and run away, but he didn't. His head dropped again, and for a second he rested it on my shoulder. I stroked his leathery nose, and whispered, "Well done. I was scared before I met you, you know...REALLY scared. We all get frightened sometimes. Just pretend you're feeling brave, and it'll be fine."

I went on walking, and to my astonishment I heard clapping and cheering on either side of us. A moment later King Percival came puffing up smiling the most ENORMOUS smile.

"That was VERY well done, Princess Lucy!" he said. "Very well done indeed! Goodness! Whoever could have been stupid enough to scream like that? If

Valiant had run away we'd have
had REAL trouble!"

Fairy G came striding out of the
crowd. "I think, King Percival,"
she said grimly, "there's no doubt
at all as to who was behind this
silly trick!" And she pointed.

Everyone turned to stare—
And there was Diamonde, blushing scarlet.

"I saw a wasp," she began, but Gruella gave her a sharp push.

"I TOLD you not to scream, Diamonde! You NEVER listen to me!"

"Princess Diamonde!" Fairy G's voice was almost as loud as Valiant's roar. "Please come here and explain yourself!"

I don't know what Diamonde said, but I don't suppose for a moment she admitted she was trying to get Lily Room into trouble. She must have been sent back to Pearl Palace, though, because we didn't see her again.

We went on with the parade, right up to the silver gates of the Home for Ancient Dragons.

The most enormous ribbon was stretched across the doorway, and Hannah and I were the princesses

who actually cut it, while
Sarah, Ellie, Grace and Isabella
held it up so everyone could see.

As soon as it was cut we announced the home was open, and led the dragons inside – and it was SO lovely! They were so

happy to be in a cosy warm
building they almost purred, and
Valiant curled up at once on the
fresh golden straw.

"I do hope you enjoy it here," I told him, and I made the old dragon my very best curtsey. "Have a very Happy Christmas, Lord Valiant."

Chapter Six

There was a sudden burst of trumpets, and a pageboy appeared in the doorway.

"King Percival's compliments, and the Christmas Ball is about to begin!" he announced.

Hannah and I stared at each other. "A Christmas Ball?" I asked in surprise.

Fairy G chuckled loudly. "That's right," she said. "But we kept it as a surprise. A Christmas Ball – and Lily Room have one more task to do today."

"What's that?" we asked.

"You have to dance the opening dance!" Fairy G told us.

And do you know what? We did dance the opening dance – and every other dance as well. It was GLORIOUS!

And at the very end, when we couldn't dance another step, the coaches rolled up to take us home...and each coach was hung with twinkling ribbons.

"Oh – what a wonderful wonderful day and night," Grace sighed as we collapsed on the soft velvet cushions.

Grace was right...

And do you know what? It was ESPECIALLY wonderful because you were there too.

See you at Emerald Castle!

Win a Tiara Club
Perfect Princess Prize!

There are six tiaras hidden in *Princess Parade*,
and each one has a secret word in it
in mirror writing. Find all six words and
re-arrange them to make a special Perfect Princess
sentence, then send it to us. Each month, we will
put the correct entries in a draw and one lucky
reader will receive a magical Perfect Princess Prize!

Send your Perfect Princess sentence, your name
and your address on a postcard to:
THE TIARA CLUB COMPETITION,
Orchard Books, 338 Euston Road,
London, NW1 3BH

Australian readers should write to:
Hachette Children's Books,
Level 17/207 Kent Street, Sydney, NSW 2000.

Only one entry per child.
Final draw: October 2008

By Vivian French

The Tiara Club

The Tiara Club at Silver Towers

The Tiara Club at Ruby Mansions

The Tiara Club at Pearl Palace

PRINCESS HANNAH AND THE LITTLE BLACK KITTEN	ISBN	978 1 84616 498 9
PRINCESS ISABELLA AND THE SNOW-WHITE UNICORN	ISBN	978 1 84616 499 6
PRINCESS LUCY AND THE PRECIOUS PUPPY	ISBN	978 1 84616 500 9
PRINCESS GRACE AND THE GOLDEN NIGHTINGALE	ISBN	978 1 84616 501 6
PRINCESS ELLIE AND THE ENCHANTED FAWN	ISBN	978 1 84616 502 3
PRINCESS SARAH AND THE SILVER SWAN	ISBN	978 1 84616 503 0

Coming soon: The Tiara Club at Emerald Castle

PRINCESS AMELIA AND THE SILVER SEAL	ISBN	978 1 84616 869 7
PRINCESS LEAH AND THE GOLDEN SEAHORSE	ISBN	978 1 84616 870 3
PRINCESS RUBY AND THE ENCHANTED WHALE	ISBN	978 1 84616 871 0
PRINCESS MILLIE AND THE MAGICAL MERMAID	ISBN	978 1 84616 872 7
PRINCESS RACHEL AND THE DANCING DOLPHIN	ISBN	978 1 84616 873 4
PRINCESS ZOE AND THE WISHING SHELL	ISBN	978 1 84616 874 1
CHRISTMAS WONDERLAND	ISBN	978 1 84616 296 1
PRINCESS PARADE	ISBN	978 1 84616 504 7
BUTTERFLY BALL	ISBN	978 1 84616 470 5

All priced at £3.99.
Christmas Wonderland, *Princess Parade* and *Butterfly Ball* are priced at £5.99.
The Tiara Club books are available from all good bookshops, or can be ordered direct
from the publisher: Orchard Books, PO BOX 29, Douglas IM99 1BQ
Credit card orders please telephone 01624 836000 or fax 01624 837033 or visit our
website: www.wattspub.co.uk or e-mail: bookshop@enterprise.net for details.

To order please quote title, author, ISBN and your full name and address.
Cheques and postal orders should be made payable to 'Bookpost plc.'
Postage and packing is FREE within the UK
(overseas customers should add £2.00 per book).

Prices and availability are subject to change.

Check out

website at:

www.tiaraclub.co.uk

You'll find Perfect Princess games and fun things to do, as well as news on the Tiara Club and all your favourite princesses!